What Kids Say About
Carole Marsh Mysteries . . .

I love the real locations! Reading the book always makes me want to go and visit them all on our next family vacation. My Mom says maybe, but I can't wait!

One day, I want to be a real kid in one of Ms. Marsh's mystery books. I think it would be fun, and I think I am a real character anyway. I filled out the application and sent it in. I hope they pick me!

History was not my favorite subject till I started reading Carole Marsh Mysteries. Ms. Marsh really brings history to life. Also, she leaves room for the scary and fun.

I think the characters are so smart and brave. They are lucky because they get to do so much cool stuff! I always wish I could be right there with them!

The kids in the story are cool and funny! They make me laugh a lot! I like that there ar of different ages. Some mysteries find a favorite character to iden

They are scary, but not too scar a lot. There is always food, which makes me hungry. I feel like I am there.*

What Parents and Teachers Say About Carole Marsh Mysteries . . .

I think kids love these books because they have such a wealth of detail. I know I learn a lot reading them! It's an engaging way to look at the history of any place or event. I always say I'm only going to read one chapter to the kids, but that never happens—it's always two or three, at least!
—Librarian

Reading the mystery and going on the field trip—Scavenger Hunt in hand—was the most fun our class ever had! It really brought the place and its history to life. They loved the real kids characters and all the humor. I loved seeing them learn that reading is an experience to enjoy!
 —4th grade teacher

Carole Marsh is really on to something with these unique mysteries. They are so clever; kids want to read them all. The Teacher's Guides are chock full of activities, recipes, and additional fascinating information. My kids thought I was an expert on the subject—and with this tool, I felt like it!
—3rd grade teacher

My students loved writing their own mystery book! Ms. Marsh's reproducible guidelines are a real jewel. They learned about copyright and more & ended up with their own book they were so proud of!
 —Reading/Writing Teacher

"The kids seem very realistic—my children seemed to relate to the characters. Also, it is educational by expanding their knowledge about the famous places in the books."

"They are what children like: mysteries and adventures with children they can relate to."

"Encourages reading for pleasure."

"This series is great. It can be used for reluctant readers, and as a history supplement."

Dear Bats:

The Creepy Cave Caper Mystery

By Carole Marsh

Published by Gallopade International/Carole Marsh Books. Printed
in the United States of America.

Managing Editor: Sherry Moss
Senior Editor: Janice Baker
Assistant Editor: Mike Kelly
Cover Design and Illustrations: Yvonne Ford
Cover images: ©Ralf Kraft. Image from BigStockPhoto.com,
©Slavoljub Pantelic. Image from BigStockPhoto.com

Gallopade International is introducing SAT words that kids need to
know in each new book tht we publish. The SAT words are bold in the
story. Look for this special logo 🔲 beside each word.

Gallopade is proud to be a member and supporter of these
educational organizations and associations:
                American Booksellers Association
                American Library Association
                International Reading Association
                National Association for Gifted Children
        The National School Supply and Equipment Association
            The National Council for the Social Studies
                    Museum Store Association
                Association of Partners for Public Lands

20 Years Ago . . .

As a mother and an author, one of the fondest periods of my life was when I decided to write mystery books for children. At this time (1979) kids were pretty much glued to the TV, something parents and teachers complained about the way they do about web surfing and blogging today.

I decided to set each mystery in a real place—a place kids could go and visit for themselves after reading the book. And I also used real children as characters. Usually a couple of my own children served as characters, and I had no trouble recruiting kids from the book's location to also be characters.

Also, I wanted all the kids—boys and girls of all ages—to participate in solving the mystery. And, I wanted kids to learn something as they read. Something about the history of the location. And I wanted the stories to be funny. That formula of real+scary+smart+fun served me well.

I love getting letters from teachers and parents who say they read the book with their class or child, then visited the historic site and saw all the places in the mystery for themselves. What's so great about that? What's great is that you and your children have an experience that bonds you together forever. Something you shared. Something you both cared about at the time. Something that crossed all age levels—a good story, a good scare, a good laugh!

20 years later,

Carole Marsh

Christina "Mystery Girl" Mimi Papa Grant

Hey, kids! As you see, here we are ready to embark on another of our exciting Carole Marsh Mystery adventures. My grandchildren often travel with me all over the world as I research new books. We have a great time together, and learn things we will carry with us for the rest of our lives!

I hope you will go to www.carolemarshmysteries.com and explore the many Carole Marsh Mysteries series!

Well, the *Mystery Girl* is all tuned up and ready for "take-off!" Gotta go...Papa says so! Wonder what I've forgotten this time?

Happy "Armchair Travel" Reading,

Mimi

P.S. Send <u>me</u> a postcard...and receive a postcard from a...**<u>BAT!</u>**

About the Characters

Paul Post is the postmaster of the post office in Postcard, Pennsylvania. He's quiet, soft-spoken and a bit of a worrywart. He's not a whiz at electronics, but can hold his own. He hates to drive, and doesn't always like to be the one in charge.

Penelope Post is a street-smart, independent mother with her own postcard company. She doesn't know much about technology, and likes to run around in curlers and sweat clothes. She loves homeschooling her children and taking trips, because every trip is an education you can't get in books.

Peter Post inherited his mother's love for traveling. He's an 11-year old who loves to figure out puzzles, riddles, and a good mystery, of course. Peter never goes anywhere without his backpack, which contains his laptop and spy paraphernalia.

Piper Post inherited her mother's sassiness. She's a very smart 10-year-old, but doesn't like school very much. Piper loves her adventures with her brother and usually uncovers the last bit of information to help Peter solve the mystery. She also loves to tell **KNOCK-KNOCK** jokes, just to annoy Peter!

Books in This Series

Table of Contents

Travel with the Post Family

Postcard, Pennsylvania

Fort Knox, Kentucky

Mammoth Cave

Prologue

A *faint streak of streetlight squeezed around the blinds of the only window in the room. It landed upon a book about the adventures of Huckleberry Finn. Peter Post laid perfectly still, except for the rapid activity beneath his closed eyelids, his mind* **oblivious** *to the creeks and groans of their old house. His eyes darted about searching, like radar, for a memory. Peter's eye movements gradually slowed.*

Scenes sped past his mind's eye registering themselves at the front of his mind, like old movies on a dull screen, and then moved on. An image of him lying in green grass morphed into an image of a cave. He was hungry and tired. He could see the weariness in his eyes as he wandered in the darkness. Then the image mutated and began moving again. His mind dove deeply into a dream.

Peter saw himself racing through the cave, as he felt the fear of being alone. His rapid eye movement sped up, and his heart started to pound in his chest. Sweat dripped down his face onto his pillow. His body jerked and his legs moved restlessly under the covers.

The sound of rushing water captured his mind; he was suspended over it. Suddenly, his body dropped through the air, plunging deep into the water. His head sprung out of the water, as the current pushed him along. He reached out to grab a rope stretched across the water. He yanked the upper half of his body free of its grip, but found he couldn't move his right arm. It held something tightly in its grasp. It was his younger sister, Piper. He couldn't pull them both free from the water's deadly current before it plucked him off the rope. It was over.

Peter bolted out of bed, gasping for air. He stood and paced around the room, trying to relax. The dream was fading fast into distant memory. He walked down the hall and rinsed off his face with cold water. He stood there a few seconds, staring at himself in the mirror, trying to remember the dream. He could remember a cave, and something to do with water. It was like he had been an acrobat in a circus, but instead of a safety net, there was water.

"Man, I've got to stop reading weird stories before going to sleep!" Peter went back to his room. His pillow was up against the headboard where he expected to find it. He pulled it down an arm's length. He'd discovered that if he slept lower in his bed, he didn't have bad dreams.

After drifting off to sleep again, his subconscious mind saw bats racing toward him...

I Vant to Suck Your Blood

Piper jumped out of *Breadloaf*, their bread-loaf-shaped, 1968, 26-foot, silver Airstream Overlander tow-along trailer, slamming the screen door behind her. "I'll be back in a minute," she said. "Mom has one more box that needs to come out."

"Okay," Peter said. "Take your time, Dad's not home yet."

As Piper disappeared into the house, Peter peered at the purple night sky. Lightning flashed, streaking randomly between the clouds and down to the ground. He loved electrical storms.

Peter scooped up the last box of supplies to carry out to *Breadloaf*.

⚡ *CRACK!* ⚡

Standing just inside the opening of the garage, his thoughts drifted back a few months to their trip to Area 51. Lightning like this would forever remind him of their trip into the desert that night. It was like they had viewed a piece of the future.

Maybe this vacation trip to Kentucky will bring some excitement back into my life, Peter thought. Life in Postcard, Pennsylvania was pretty dull, and caves and bats were awesome, after all. He had brought up some Internet sites on Kentucky's caves. Although most of them were all the same—with walking tours and fancy lighting—he was hoping to convince his parents to get down and get dirty. He wanted to go spelunking and climb and crawl through the more mysterious parts of caves.

CRACK! Lightning had hit something in the distance, as other bolts crackled across the sky. He hadn't seen an awesome electrical storm like this since the year before last. Even if this trip was not as good as the last one, it would still be great to get away. He figured his dad wouldn't want to drive through an electrical storm. But his mom would; she'd drive through a minefield with a sledgehammer in her hand! If they got started soon, they might possibly be able to **elude** the rain.

He hopped on board *Breadloaf*. He walked to the back bedroom and stuffed the box in an overhead compartment. He then reached inside the side closet and pulled out the mask and black cape he had gotten from a friend. He quickly pulled the rubber mask over his head and positioned it so he could see clearly through the eyeholes. After putting on the cape, he hid in the bathroom.

A minute later, Piper sprang up into *Breadloaf* with a box in her hand. She went to put it in the back bedroom when Peter jumped out of the bathroom with his hands high in the air.

"I vant to suck your blood!" he yelled, seeing a reflection of his Dracula mask in the closet mirror.

"AAAAHHHH!!!!" Piper screamed, louder than Peter had ever heard before. She lurched, throwing the box into the air, scattering its contents everywhere. She turned and bolted from the trailer. Lightning flashed in front of her. She screamed even louder.

Peter chased her as he yelled, "I vant to suck your blood, little girl, because you drive me batty!"

A pickup truck backing up the driveway to the garage stopped just in time before Piper bounded past it. Peter's dad jumped out. "What are you two doing?" he asked.

"Nothing Dad, but I vant to suck your blood," Peter said, lumbering toward his father.

"Not until you and Piper finish unloading these two boxes of school supplies for your mom," Dad said, pointing to the boxes in the pickup, while ignoring Peter's costume.

"Okay," Peter said, yanking off his mask and cape. He stuffed them behind some cans of paint on one of the shelves.

"It's kind of ironic," Dad said. "We're heading off to Kentucky, and those two boxes just arrived from Kentucky."

Piper had run around and inside the house. She cautiously opened the door between the house and the garage and stuck her head out. "Is the vampire still here?" she asked.

"*What vampire?*" Peter and his dad asked together.

Bat Banter

"Help your brother unload the pickup," Dad said.

Piper batted her eyes at her dad. "Who, me?" she asked sweetly.

"You can do it, girl. Where's your mom?" her father said.

"Mixing up some pancake batter for the trip," said Piper.

"Okay," Dad said. "When you get done out here check all the windows and batten down the house."

"Hey Dad, did you get some batteries for the flashlights?" Peter asked.

"Yeah," Dad said. "Are we all loaded up and ready to go?"

"Uh huh!" Piper said. "Except for the batting that Mom wanted to bring along for the couch pillows she's making."

"Okay," Dad said. "I'll take care of that. Can you guys do me a favor? You know how you always get a bit batty before a trip? Can you just kind of chill, I've had a busy day and I'm beat up and battered."

"Sure, Dad," Peter said. "While we're driving, Piper and I will just bat around some ideas about things we want to do on the trip."

"Great!" Dad said. He noticed Piper holding her new baton. "Are you bringing that?"

"No," she said. "I was going to use it as a battering ram against that blood-sucking vampire!"

"Oh, okay," Dad said, leaping the two stairs into the house.

Peter and Piper each grabbed a box and carried it to the back of the garage. As Peter slid his box onto a shelf, a card fell from the bottom of the box.

Piper saw it before Peter. She handed her box to Peter and picked up the card.

"What's this?" she asked, turning it over in her hand. It was a postcard.

"What's what?" Peter said.

"It's a postcard with a riddle. It fell off of the bottom of your box," Piper said, handing Peter the postcard.

"That's weird," Peter said. "It must have gotten stuck to the bottom of the box at the post office in Kentucky."

"Isn't that a picture of the place we're going to?" Piper asked.

Peter flipped the card over. "As a matter of fact, it is! It's a picture of a cave called Mammoth Cave. Dad wants to go there. The guy who wrote this, wrote it in pencil," Peter noted.

"Wow, how do you already know a *guy* wrote it?" Piper said.

Peter looked up and smiled. "It's quite simple, my dear sister. I scoured the card for a return address, and although most of that side of the card is scratched up, including part of the cave picture, I can faintly see the name Tom."

"Oh," Piper said. "Where was the card going?"

"I don't know, that part's not legible," said Peter. "But the message side is easy enough to read. It's a pretty cool riddle."

Dear Bats,

Years have past the country doesn't know, the story was told a long time ago.

The river winds through this cavern of shame, they made it not far, the earth was to blame.

The riches weren't theirs but that was okay, because God may giveth but he taketh away.

Myth can be fact the Indians do claim. Follow their lead for fortune and fame.

Look for the treasure where a dead man last sat. Find him hidden with the eyes of a bat.

Honey, solve the riddle and I'll see you soon, Dad.
P.S. There's a hint on this postcard.

"Sounds cool, but who in the world would name their kid Bats? That's cruel and unusual punishment if you ask me," said Piper. "Bell, Buffy, and Bianca I can understand—but Bats!"

Peter scratched the top of his head. "You got me. Some people just have strange names, if you know what I mean." Piper didn't see the smirk on Peter's face.

"How would Bats go about finding the right cave?" Piper asked.

"Ha!" Peter said. "Are you suggesting, my dear Piper, that a mystery is afoot? Because if you are, I will have to concur."

"You'll have to conquer what?" Piper asked.

"Not conquer, *concur*! It means, I agree with you," Peter said, shaking his head. "Never mind! I thought this was going to be a boring trip. But this postcard is our ticket to adventure."

"Oh no!" Piper said. "Here we go again. I just hope it doesn't involve anything *creepy* this time."

Hey Kids,
Don't forget to send Carole Marsh
a postcard . . . and get one back . . .
from a pen pal BAT!

Knox-Knox, Who's There?

Peter was surprised by the size of the famous Fort Knox, their first stop in Kentucky. The word Fort conjured up, at least in his mind, a large square area, high wooden walls, and guard towers on each corner. This place was a huge Army base!

Now, from what he was reading, he was standing in the United States Bullion Depository where the government kept billions of dollars in

gold and other precious metals. The depository
was located at Fort Knox.

"Knox-Knox," Piper said.

"Not again," Peter said. "This is your third
corny **Knock-Knock** joke in the last hour."

"My Knox-Knox jokes aren't corny," Piper
said. *"Knox-Knox!"*

"Okay!" Peter said. "Who's there?"

"This is," said Piper.

"This is who?" Peter asked.

"This is boring," Piper said.

"No it's not," Peter replied. "The only thing
boring are your Knox-Knox jokes."

"Yes, Fort Knox is boring," Piper argued.

"No it isn't," Peter said. "Besides, Dad's gone
places for you without complaining. Why can't
you do the same for him?"

"Okay!   Okay!   You're right," Piper said,
looking across the room at her parents, who
seemed to be enjoying their visit. She liked the
color of her mother's scarf.   The green
highlighted her pink curlers. Plus, it matched
her sweats.

"But why would he want to visit this place?"
Piper asked. "It's not like we get to see all the
gold.   It's buried in vaults in the basement.

Speaking of which, doesn't the government recommend that you put your money in a bank instead of burying it in your mattress? They should take their own advice. This place is nothing but a big concrete mattress."

Peter shook his head. "Why don't you try to learn something? This place was built in 1936, and in the spring of 1937 the government started bringing gold here." Peter flipped through the brochure. "See, here's something else that's cool. Besides gold, documents like the *Declaration of Independence*, the *U.S. Constitution*, and the *Magna Carta* were stored here during World War II."

Not far from Peter and Piper, a short, old, rail-thin man stood looking at one of the displays.

"Is that right?! Wow, that's like priceless information!" Piper teased. "What's the *Magna Carta* anyway?"

"It's the most significant man-made document ever written!" the old man said. "I'm sorry, but I couldn't help but overhear your conversation. The *Magna Carta* led to the rule of constitutional law today. Plus, it influenced many other documents, like our *Constitution*. It's considered one of the most important documents in history."

"Cool," Piper said. "But that's still boring."

The old man laughed. "Well, let's see. What can I tell you that isn't boring? How about the fact that many people have wanted to steal the gold buried, as you say, in this giant concrete mattress, but only one attempt has ever succeeded."

That got their attention!

Stolen Treasure

"No way!" Peter said. "Everything I've read about the Depository is that it's impenetrable. No one has ever been able to break into it."

"How would they move all that gold?" Piper asked. "It weighs a ton."

"First," the old man said, "do you think the government would tell us that gold was stolen from such an impenetrable place as this?" The old man waved his hands about. "The Feds would keep it a secret."

Piper's eyes were fixed on the old man. "You mean someone..."

"No," the old man said. "As far as I know, no one has ever broken into the vaults."

Peter and Piper looked disappointed.

"But, the year I lived in Kentucky, I heard a rumor that two men, helping to transport the first shipment of gold to Fort Knox, managed to run off with a small fortune in gold coins before it arrived here," the old man said. "No one knows for sure what kind of gold coins they were, but in today's market they would be priceless.

"Supposedly," he continued, "they got away with the gold and were never heard from again. The government never admitted that it ever happened."

"You mean no one ever found them?" Piper asked.

"Duh!" Peter said. "That's what, *never heard from again* means. Were there any other rumors about the stolen gold?"

"Just the usual stuff made of myths and legends," the old man said. "The stories over the years have run the gamut from the men making it to South America where they lived like kings, to them dying by the hand of a federal marshal who took the gold and disappeared. Another story says they loaded the gold onto several horses, and headed south to hide in the caves until the coast was clear."

"Cool!" Piper said, looking at Peter.

"Which tale do you think is true?" Peter asked.

"Hmm," the old man said. "I don't know; I'd like to think that they never got away, and that the gold is still hidden nearby. Well, I've got to go now. You children enjoy your visit. Just think, there aren't too many children who can claim they stood over a mattress with billions of dollars in gold buried in it." The old man tilted his hat as he left.

"Thanks!" Peter said, watching the man walk away.

"Where's the riddle?" Piper asked.

"Right here," Peter pulled the postcard from his back pocket.

Piper looked at it. "Are you thinking what I'm thinking?" Piper asked.

Peter looked at the card again. "I hate to admit it, but yeah. The treasure in the riddle could be the stolen gold. It would fit if the men took the gold into the caves."

"Do you think it could be in Mammoth Cave, where we're going?" Piper asked.

"I don't know," Peter replied. "But I have a hunch it could be!" He flipped the card over. "You know that hint the writer of the postcard mentioned? It's right in front of us!" Peter held up the picture of Mammoth Cave.

"Knox-Knox."

Peter shook his head. "Who's there?"

"Spell."

"Spell who?" Peter asked.

"Spelunking we will go, spelunking we will go. High, ho, the merry-o, spelunking we will go!" Piper sang and laughed, as she skipped ahead of Peter.

Riddle Me This!

"Your Mom and I are going to run to the store," Dad said, as he finished disconnecting the SUV from *Breadloaf*. "You guys finish setting up the campsite and we'll be back soon, okay?"

"If you get done before we get back, don't wander too far away," Mom instructed, straightening a loose pink curler above her forehead. "When we get back we'll make some dinner on the grill."

The SUV pulled away as Peter and Piper started setting up camp. Peter hooked up all the exterior fittings for water, sewage, and electricity, while Piper put up their screened dining tent. Together, they unpacked the outside furniture and stored the supplies they had brought. Then they hauled out the grill. Peter connected the grill's propane line, while Piper set up a work table next to it.

When they were done, Peter stood back and inspected everything. Peter didn't like to be **negligent** in his duties. He always triple-checked everything he did.

Piper sprang off the step from *Breadloaf* and almost bowled her brother over. "Do you think the old man back at Fort Knox was pulling our leg?" Piper asked.

"It's possible he **embellished** the story a bit," Peter admitted. "Let's run to the trading post. I want to see if they have anything on caves in the area."

They reached the store and split up. As Peter headed for the book and magazine shelves, Piper scooted around the store, not searching for anything, but eyeballing everything. She liked to check out the campsite, or trading post store, as Peter called it, to see what they had. She was looking off to the side when she bumped into a girl, almost knocking her over. She caught the girl by the arm. "I'm so sorry. I didn't see you there."

The girl straightened herself. "That's okay. As my grandma, Morningstar, says, I'm just a wisp of a girl. My little brother is bigger than me and he's three years younger. My name is Segura Broadfoot," she said, holding out her hand.

Piper shook it. "Hi, Segura, I'm Piper Post. Are you an American Indian?"

"Let's see," Segura said. "What gave it away, my name, my grandma's name, or the pigtails I'm wearing?"

Piper giggled. "All of it. I love your pigtails. Would you be able to show me how to do that?"

"I'm not real good at it, but my grandma is, and I'm sure she wouldn't mind doing yours," Segura said. "Are you camping here?"

"Yeah! We just got here with our parents," Piper replied. "That's my brother Peter over there. We'll be here for a week. How about you?"

"I live here year-round," Segura said. "My grandfather is the groundskeeper. We live in a trailer on the other side of the property."

Piper saw Peter walking toward the door. "I've got to get back to our trailer. Do you think it'll be okay for my brother and I to come by after dinner?"

"Sure," Segura said. "My grandma likes it when people drop in. If you have a favorite brush, bring it with you. Oh! Be prepared to hear a lot of stories. My grandfather could write an encyclopedia about life in Kentucky. They've lived here all their lives. He acts sort of batty, sometimes, but some of his stories are real creepy and will give you goosebumps!"

The Birds and The Bees

Mom glanced at the wall clock above the couch. It was a little after six in the evening or 6:00 post-meridian, as Peter liked to say.

Peter had already finished eating and was sitting by a window pointing a small ray-gun-looking device at his father and a group of people down at the campground swimming pool.

"Here's your soda, Mom," Piper said.

Peter turned from the window, excited. "Mom, Piper, check this out! It's awesome!" he shouted. He removed the ear buds from his ears and offered one to each of them.

His mother thought it was going to be a song he liked, but instead she heard her husband talking about the campground swimming pool.

Peter held up the device with a flattened clear plastic dish and a black handle. "It's a parabolic listening device. I call it my 'listening post.' I can listen to sounds up to 150 feet away."

"Who are you?" Mom asked. "The FBI or the CIA, and what have you done with my son?"

"The name is Post, Peter Post," Peter replied.

"Where on earth did you get that thing?" Mom asked.

"I built it from the spy kit you and Dad gave me for Christmas," Peter said. "It's great for listening to birds, and bees buzzing around their hives, and the occasional suspicious conversation. You just never know when it may come in handy."

Mom eyed him. "Okay, but don't do anything illegal with it. Remember, a real man uses his brain and doesn't break the law ever!"

"Come on, Mom, you know me better than that," Peter said, moving his eyebrows up and down to tease her.

"Why did you put our name on it?" Mom asked, pointing to the handle of the device.

Peter laughed. "That's not our name," he said. "P.O.S.T. stands for Power On Self Test. That's what this push button switch does." Peter pointed to the switch below the word P.OS.T. "When it powers up, it runs a simple test of the circuits."

"You never cease to amaze me," Mom said.

"You don't know him like I do," Piper said. "Or you'd be over that, Mom."

Suddenly, her brother's eyes got wide and Piper could tell he was hearing something *very interesting*!

Information Junkie

"Segura said you've lived in this part of Kentucky all your lives," Peter said to Segura's grandfather, when they went to visit after dinner. "I don't mean to be rude, but I heard grandma Morningstar call you WB. What does that stand for?"

"Well, my given name is William Broadfoot," WB said. "But when I was about your age, I loved to roam the caves in the area and study the bats. My father said that when he watched me play around the caves, I was as wild as the bats I played with. Pretty soon he started calling me WildBat and it stuck! Over time, my friends shortened it to WB, which, ironically, fits my real initials."

"That's awesome!" Peter said.

"Whoa!" Piper said. "You played with bats? Bats are disgusting! When their icky-looking wings are folded up and their mouths are closed they kind of look cute, like little mice. But once they open their mouths or spread their wings—yuck!"

"I've held many bats and have studied them all my life," WB said. "Bats wouldn't make good pets, but I've had some live in captivity with me for short periods of time."

"He's a bat expert," Morningstar said. "He's known around these parts for his bat expertise. Anyone who needs information about bats comes to him. I like to say that I'm married to the real Batman."

"Now that's awesome!" Peter said. "I know that although there are over 1,000 different species of bats, we only have 40 species in America. Most bats live in tropical forests and bats don't live in extreme cold areas or hot deserts. I also know that most bats aren't blind. And even though some bats have poor vision, many of them can see clearly. But they use echolocation to find food and to keep from bumping into things. The bat makes a high-pitched sound, and the sound waves bounce off

of something and come back to the bat's ears. If I remember right, bats are colorblind, though."

"That's good," WB said. He turned toward Morningstar. "Maybe I have a successor here."

Morningstar laughed. "Maybe you should nickname him Robin."

"If he's Robin, I get to be Batgirl," Piper said.

"What else do you know about bats?" WB asked.

"Hmm, let's see," Peter said. "Some bats live in caves, barns, or old buildings, while other bats live in trees. Most bats eat insects. Some eat fruit, and a few eat small creatures like birds, frogs, mice, or even small fish. Vampire bats," Peter looked at his sister and bared his teeth like a vampire, "live in South America, not North America, and they hardly ever bite humans. They attack animals that are sleeping, like cows or goats."

"If you ask me you've got bats in your belfry," Piper said. "Peter didn't know any of this until a week ago. When we get ready to go on a trip, he reads everything about the place we're going. It's like having your own tourist guide in your family."

"So sue me!" Peter said. "I'm an information junkie. I just like to know what I'm getting myself into. I once read that it's better to have knowledge and never use it, than to not have that knowledge and need to use it."

"Hmm," Morningstar said. "Now you are sounding like WB here. He likes to say that we gather knowledge from the ancient spirits for the challenges in life. Without that knowledge, the ancients say we are lost."

"My grandfather tried to teach me many things," WB began in a slow, deep voice, "such as the ways of the ancients, including some of our tribal myths. I've learned since that many myths have their basis in fact. Most of what he tried to teach me I thought was out-dated, a waste of time.

"The world was becoming a modern place," he continued. "I thought I would never need to use any of the things he taught me. The old ways of our forefathers were being left behind. Then one day when I was a boy of ten, I wandered into a cave just to check it out. I loved it. So, I made a torch and went deeper and deeper into the cave.

"I had just gone through a large cavern, which wasn't as beautiful as the first, when I heard somebody in the cave behind me. A few seconds later the ground shook—and I found myself trapped!"

Caves Are Not Just For Cavemen

Piper sat mesmerized by WB's story, as grandma Morningstar finished the last braid in her pigtails. "How did you get trapped?" Piper asked.

"A cave-in had closed off the large cavern from the tunnel I was in," WB said.

"What did you do?" Piper asked.

"I panicked," WB said. "My heart felt like it would pound out of my chest. What was I going to do? I was trapped! I would surely die without anyone knowing where I was. My grandfather's voice came back to me. The stuff that had sounded so simple-minded to me before started rattling around my mind, calming me, giving me faith and strength."

"How did you find your way out?" Peter asked.

"I walked further into the cave, and as I arrived at another smaller cavern, I listened to my grandfather's voice," WB said. "My grandfather had told me how our ancestors had used the caves in ancient times. In order to find their way in and out of the caves, they would etch one of two symbols into the cave walls just above the floor."

"What did they mean?" Piper asked.

"One symbol marked their secret passages that led to other caves they didn't want anyone else to find. It meant *cave within a cave*. But in all the time I spent in the caves, I never came upon one of those symbols." WB took a piece of paper and drew the symbol on it. It was a large circle surrounding a smaller circle.

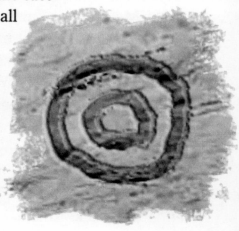

"But it was the other symbol that saved my life," WB said, as he drew the symbol. It was also a large circle, but instead of having another smaller circle, it had a line that went from the inside of the circle to the outside. 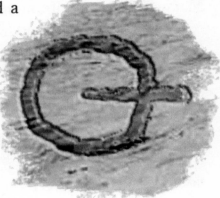 "I followed those symbols toward a small hidden exit just 100 feet down the cave. I managed to wiggle and squirm my way through a long hole to freedom and cool afternoon air.

"That day was one of the most **harrowing** experiences of my life, but it taught me what I wouldn't let my grandfather teach me."

"What was that?" Piper asked.

"That all knowledge is useful," WB said. "Knowledge is like a buffet table. You should grab a little of everything. After that experience, I learned a lot from my grandfather, right up until the day he died."

"Do you know what cave you were in?" Peter asked.

"Oh, yes," WB answered. "It was Mammoth Cave, one of the most famous in the world!"

Peter and Piper looked at each other. "Is Mammoth Cave far from here?" Peter asked.

"Nope!" WB said. "You're just about there."

"Good!" Piper said. "We can't wait to crawl around in a cave—at least Peter can't!"

"Do you think we can get a special tour of Mammoth Cave?" Peter asked. "I mean, I know they give tours every day, but we want to see the cool passageways most people don't see."

WB nodded his head. "I'm sure that my friend Tom Bradley, the head park ranger, would be happy to take you on a tour," he assured them. "He loves it when kids are really interested in his cave. I'll call him in the morning. I should let you know that a lot of people in the area think Tom's a little batty, but I think he's an upstanding guy for a paleface."

"Why do they think he's loony?" Piper asked.

"Well," WB said. "Tom's been searching Mammoth Cave for years. He believes there's a hidden treasure buried there."

Peter and Piper looked at each other and smiled. "Do you know if Mr. Bradley has any kids?" Peter asked.

"Yes, he has a daughter who's in college somewhere," WB said, looking at Morningstar. "What's her name again?"

"Battina!" Morningstar said. "As I recall, his pet name for her is Bats."

Now Peter and Piper *really* looked at each other—and grinned!

The Plan

Peter and Piper walked along the trail leading back to *Breadloaf*. "I can't believe that we've already discovered the writer of the postcard," Peter said.

"You know what Mom says," Piper began. "There's no such thing as *can't*. It's either I don't want to or I'm not able to!"

"Okay," Peter said. "I'm not able to believe that we've already discovered the writer of the postcard. Is that better?"

"Much!" Piper said. "Mom would be proud."

Peter pulled the postcard from his pocket and tapped the picture of Mammoth Cave. "That's were Tom or Mr. Bradley believes the gold is buried."

"Do you think he's found it yet?" Piper asked.

"Naw!" Peter replied. "If he had, he wouldn't have included the riddle for his daughter. I'll bet the riddle is a game between the two of them, like when Dad leaves little clues around the house for us to find."

"Now all we have to do is convince Mom and Dad to let us take the special tour," Peter said. "Then we can look for the treasure while we're crawling around."

"Okay, Robin," Piper said. "You're the crime-solver and defender of the weak, along with being a bat expert. I want to know how you're going to use your skills to get our parents to agree. You know Mom's not fond of caves or bats and Dad likes those boring guided tours."

"The key, my dear Batgirl, is Mom. If Mom wants to do something else, Dad will follow," Peter said. "And what's the key to getting Mom to change her mind?"

Piper stopped dead in her tracks and smiled. "EDUCATION!" she said.

The Wonders of Mineral Water!

The next day, the Post family(plus their new friend Segura) made their way to Mammoth Cave.

"See!" Dad said, watching tourists line up at the cave entrance. "That's the tour we should be on!"

"Honey, the kids will learn more from Mr. Bradley than some teenage guide in a fancy lit-up cavern. Besides, it's an education just waiting to happen," Mom said, waving her hand like the education part was a no-brainer. "Don't worry, we're here for a week. We'll do some things that you want to do later. Okay?"

"Okay!" Dad said, nodding his head. He changed moods quickly as Tom Bradley appeared and shook his hand in a warm greeting.

"Mr. Post," Mr. Bradley remarked, "you and your family will love my special tour! Now, I'm going to give each of you items that I like everyone to have when they enter a cave, even if they're not going spelunking."

Tom handed out bottles of water, matches, and helmets with waterproof flashlights mounted on them, plus extra batteries for the flashlights.

"This is a five-hour trek in and out of the cave, so these items will help you be prepared for the worst," Tom said. "That way you're ready for Murphy's Law. Oh, and you can all call me Tom."

No one noticed Dad's jaw drop at the mention of a five-hour trek.

"Murphy's Law?" Piper said, confused.

"Yeah!" Peter said. "Murphy's Law states that whatever can go wrong, will go wrong. It's like hanging around with you."

Before Piper could respond, Tom added, "The full law says, whatever can go wrong, will go wrong at the most inappropriate time. So even though I've never had anything go wrong, I want to make sure you have some of the items that could help you out of a jam. Okay! Let's get started. Turn on your flashlights and stay close together."

Tom led the way through the cave entrance with Piper and Segura holding hands right behind him, followed by Peter, Mom, and Dad.

"Mammoth Cave National Park is the longest cave system known in the world," Tom explained. "It became a national park in 1941.

"How many miles of passageways does it have?" Piper asked, peering at the cool, dark, underworld around her.

"More than 350 miles," Tom replied. "And new discoveries add new miles just about every year."

"Did Indians live here first?" Peter asked.

"They certainly did," Tom said. "Indian possessions like pottery, sandals, torches, and wooden bowls have been found in the cave. And as an added bonus," he continued, pausing and looking straight at Peter and Piper, "they found a mummy estimated to be about 2,000 years old!"

"That's so awesome!" Peter exclaimed. "Maybe there's other stuff in here, too," he whispered to Piper.

"Peter said the caves were formed by water. Is that true?" Piper asked.

"It sure is," Tom said. "After the huge sheets of glacial ice melted, the melt-water removed the limestone and formed the cave passages."

"Oh!" Mom said, pointing to a group of shimmering, hourglass-shaped columns. "That's pretty." One of her curlers snagged a short stalactite hanging from the ceiling, which almost ripped the curler out of her hair. It ended up hanging loosely on the back of her head.

"These are speleothems, or cave decorations made by mineral deposits," Tom said. "When mineral-filled water evaporates, after it seeps through tiny cracks in the cave's ceiling, it leaves behind a stalactite. If the water drips fast, some of the minerals are deposited onto the floor, and as it evaporates, a stalagmite grows upward. A stalagmite is usually broader than the stalactite above it. When the two meet they form columns like these." Tom waved his hand at the columns.

They crept around a bend in the tunnel. "Everybody, stop and turn off your flashlights," Tom said. Blackness enveloped everything.

No one said anything for a few seconds.

"Ouch!" Piper screamed. "Peter stop that!"

"Stop what?" Peter said. "I didn't do anything. It must have been a bat or another vampire chasing you. You know how they love to bite little girls and turn them into vampires, especially ones with pigtails."

"Yeah, well, if I become a vampire I'm coming after you," Piper said. "So you better put an iron cage around your neck or it's mine."

"Can you bite me, too?" Segura asked.

"Sure, why?" Piper replied.

"Because if I become a vampire, I can stay up all night," Segura giggled.

"Okay kids," Mom said. "My gosh, it's unbelievably dark in here. I can't even see my hand in front of my face."

"I wonder if this is how dark it was for WB when he was stuck in the cave by himself," Peter said. "Because this is pretty scary."

"Ouch!" Piper screamed again. "Peter!"

"Peter, that's enough!" Mom said as she turned on her flashlight.

Everyone looked at where Tom should have been standing.

But he wasn't there!

Stalactites or Stalagmites?

"Tom!" Mom called out.

Nothing.

"He was here just a second ago," Piper said. "Peter, did you and Tom plan this?"

"I'm right here," Tom said.

Everyone turned around. Tom was standing behind Dad at the back of the line. "How did you get back here so fast without me hearing you?" Dad asked.

"I snuck around through a side tunnel," Tom said. "There's something up here I want you to see.   I didn't want to block your view when we first see it. I know we have a couple of brave girls up there, so I thought they could lead the way."

"I don't know about Segura," Peter said. "But you don't know Piper, do you? She's scared of sleeping in a dark bedroom."

"I am not!" Piper said.

"Are too!" Peter replied.

"Am..." Piper started to say.

"Okay, let's just keep going," Mom almost shouted.

Piper and Segura stopped abruptly at the sight in front of them—a sea of shimmering stalactites hanging from the ceiling like icicles on a fir tree after a winter ice storm.

"It's so cool," Segura gasped. "Where are we?"

"The Frozen Niagara," Tom replied proudly, "one of the most beautiful places in Mammoth Cave."

Peter's light fell on a speleothem shaped like translucent draperies. Its rainbow colors reflected around the cave when the light from Peter's flashlight hit it. Everyone mulled around looking at all the incredible natural cave features.

Piper stood over a shimmering pool of color. Hanging over the pool's rim was a solid rock waterfall. Off to the side of the pool, near the wall, sat gypsum flowers and needle-shaped mineral deposits in a beautiful display made by Mother Nature. Not far from that display were some white and gold flower-like structures that seemed to ooze and curl from the wall, ceiling, and floor. It reminded Peter of the icing from a cake decorator nozzle.

"It's kind of cold in here," Mom said.

Dad removed his jacket and put it over her shoulders.

"It's not bad right now," Tom said. "The average temperature in a cave depends on the outside temperature where it's located. The caves in Minnesota are colder than our caves in Kentucky. A higher altitude will make a cave cooler also. Factors like air movement, and air pressure can add to temperature changes."

"Well," Dad said. "I'm not cold. I'm just hungry and tired from all this walking. So, I don't know about the rest of you, but this looks like a perfect place to sit down, relax, have a bite to eat, and admire the work of Mother Nature." He whipped a satchel he'd been carrying off of his shoulder. He opened it and took out two collapsible lawn chairs.

"I've got the sandwiches, honey," Mom said, opening a small cooler she'd been carrying. She sat in the chair next to her husband. "Do you kids want a sandwich?"

"Naw, I'm good," Peter said. "Vampires only drink blood or strawberry smoothies. We don't eat sandwiches."

"I'll take one," Piper said.

"Me, too!" said Segura.

Piper took the sandwiches from her mother and noticed the loose curler on the back of her mom's hair. "You've got a loose curler, let me fix it," she said, handing the sandwiches back to her mom. Piper grabbed the curler to move it back into position when suddenly a little furry head popped out from inside the curler.

"EEEKKK!"

Piper screamed, letting go of the curler and jumping back. "There's a bat in your hair!"

Bats in Mom's Belfry

Sandwiches went flying through the air as Mom jumped out of her chair. Peter had never seen his mom so frantic before. She didn't mind bugs, mice, or spiders, but he guessed bats were her limit.

"Get it out! Get it out!" Mom screamed, as she ran around the cave in a zigzag pattern screaming and waving her arms wildly. Curlers flew in every direction as she swatted at her hair trying to knock the bat free, but it clung on tight.

As she ran frantically toward the cave wall opposite the glass pool Piper had been looking at, her right foot landed in a thick layer of guano and she slid across the cave floor right toward a waist-high stalagmite. She grabbed at it to keep herself from falling into the guano and almost flew over the top of it. The sudden jolt knocked the bat free and he fluttered down the tunnel of the cave.

Mom suddenly heard laughter. Peter, Piper, and Dad were bent over, laughing hysterically. "Mom fell in bat poop!" they cried. "It's not funny!" Mom screamed.

"Oh, yes it was, dear," Dad said.

"Any major league baseball player would have admired that slide into home plate," Peter stammered, trying to get his laughter under control, but he just broke down again until even Mom, Segura, and Tom had joined in.

When they all finally slowed to snickers and giggles, Dad went over and helped Mom out of the guano and back to her seat. He used a bottle of water to rinse some of the guano off of her shoes.

"Well, I guess I've ruined lunch," she said, noticing the sandwiches sprinkled all around the cave. Her hair had only two curlers gingerly clinging to a few strands of hair. The rest of it hung in tight curls around her head.

Dad was still kneeling in front of her. "Well, I've got to admit I was wrong."

"About what?" Mom said, trying not to giggle while she combed her fingers through her hair, knocking the curlers free.

"This *is* an educational trip," he said, holding back laughter.

"Very funny, Paul," Mom said, not sounding like anything was funny at all.

Don't Worry, Be Happy!

"So, you're saying there are a lot more bats further down in the cave?" Mom asked, a rare tremble in her voice.

"Yes, there are bats, but not as many as there used to be in Mammoth Cave," Tom said. "All the tourism has affected the internal temperature in the cave, and that has affected bat hibernation."

"Well," Mom said, "if I might run into another bat...well, I think I'll just stop this tour right now and head back."

"Mom!" Peter and Piper screamed.

"We want to go further in. This is supposed to be educational," Piper said.

Peter waved at Piper and Segura. "We're not afraid of a few bats. They normally don't bother you unless you bother them. That one lone bat must have just liked your curler."

"Please, let us go!" Piper said. "If you and Dad want to head back, that's okay, Tom knows this cave. He has a cell phone, and he can call you when we're done. Please, please, please!" she begged.

Segura stepped forward. "Mrs. Post, I have been through the cave before with Tom, and Piper and Peter will learn a lot."

"Let them go, honey," Dad said.

"You're okay with this?" Mom asked. "You're the one who's the worrywart."

"Yeah, well, I guess I'm trying to learn to let go a little," Dad said. "Besides, I'm sure Tom will take good care of them." He turned toward Tom. "Won't you, Tom?"

"I'll care for them like they were me own children," he said in a lilting Irish brogue.

"Okay, it's settled then," Dad said.

"It is?" Mom asked.

"Yes, dear!" Dad said, picking up the lawn chairs, which he had already put back into their bags. "You kids have fun and call us when you get done."

Piper ran up to her dad and gave him a big hug. "Thank you, Daddy." Then she hugged her mom. "We'll be okay. Honest Injun," Piper said. "No offense!" Piper said to Segura.

"That's okay," Segura said.

Peter hugged his mom. "Don't worry, I'll take care of the girls."

"That's what Mom's worried about," Piper said.

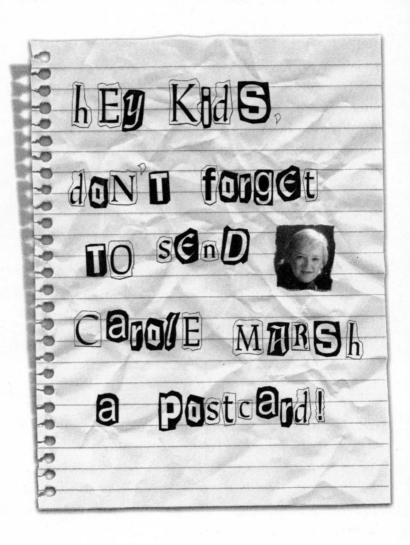

Dear Bats

Tom constantly had to stoop over to get through smaller and smaller tunnels. "We'll be coming out into another large cavern in a few minutes. Although this one isn't as pretty as the last one, we do need to be quiet so we don't disturb the bats."

"Aww, what's a few bats among friends?" Peter said. "Speaking of bats, isn't that your daughter's nickname?" he asked.

"Yes, it is," Tom said. "Her name is Battina. In another week she will be down here to visit. It's funny, but I started calling her Bats long before I got this job in Mammoth Cave National Park."

"Why do you like this cave so much?" Piper asked, just as they emerged into the large cavern.

Tom turned to look back at Piper. "Well, it's kind of a long story."

"Would it have anything to do with stolen gold from Fort Knox?" Peter asked.

Tom gazed at Peter. "How did you know that? Was WB rattling on about me?" Tom asked.

"No, well, not exactly," Peter said. "He did lead us to you, but Piper and I put together the clues."

"Clues to what?" Tom said, confused.

"It's simple," Piper said. "Our dad is the postmaster in our home town. Just before we left to go on vacation down here, Peter and I were moving boxes out of my dad's truck and we found a postcard stuck to the bottom of a box that had come from Kentucky. The postcard was one you recently sent to your daughter. But we didn't know that, because the address information on the front of the card was worn off. You wrote it in pencil, after all. All we could make out was your first name."

Peter pulled the postcard from his pocket and handed it to Tom. "You've got to admit that a message like this written to a 'Dear Bats' sounds pretty mysterious."

Tom looked over the postcard. "How did you find out I wrote it?" he asked.

"We got lucky when Piper met Segura and we were talking to WB," Peter said. "He mentioned Mammoth Cave, which is the photo on the postcard. After asking him a few questions we knew you wrote the postcard."

"Okay, but on the postcard I didn't mention anything about Fort Knox or the depository," Tom said.

"Oh! " Piper said. "I'd like to say that was some of Peter's good detective work, but we just heard the story from a man while visiting the Fort Knox Bullion Depository on our way here.

"He said the depository had never been robbed, but there was a rumor that gold was stolen when it was in route to the depository in 1937. He mentioned the theories about the disappearance of the two men that robbed the gold and after having read your postcard, the one about them holding up in caves made the most sense."

"You guys would make good detectives," Tom said.

"Do you still think there's gold buried down here?" Piper asked.

"I don't think so anymore—even though the riddle says there is," Tom said.

"You've never found anything in all the years you've been looking?" Segura said.

"No!" Tom said. "I've come to the conclusion that it's just a myth. Every year when my daughter comes to visit me for the summer, I send her a postcard with the riddle on it. It's kind of a game between the two of us."

"Where did you get the riddle?" Peter asked.

"I was a government researcher at the Department of Cultural Affairs," Tom said. "The riddle was part of the estate of Sanford Croghan. His grandfather, Dr. John Croghan, purchased Mammoth Cave in 1839. Sanford died about ten years ago. His belongings and those of some of his family came to my office to determine if there was anything worth keeping or sending to an auction.

"A few weeks after I discovered the riddle in the estate papers, I heard the rumor about the robbery. I've always been fascinated by the riddle and the cave. I've never uncovered the author of the riddle."

"Have you figured out any of the riddle?" Peter asked.

"No, just the obvious parts," Tom said, looking down at the riddle on the postcard. "The first line is simple enough to understand. But the second line is harder. I thought it might be a metaphor for something other than a river, but what else I haven't figured out. I believe the end of the second line where it says 'they made it not far, the earth was to blame' means that they got lost in the cave and couldn't find their way out."

"Could there possibly be..." Peter started to ask, when suddenly the ground shook under their feet.

Piper and Segura screamed as dust and small pebbles fell from the cavern's ceiling. Piper grabbed Segura's hand and ran a wobbly path to Peter and Tom.

The shaking stopped just as suddenly as it had started.

Peter knew what was going to happen next. "Get down!" he shouted, as he covered both girls as best as he could.

Tom quickly pulled a two-man tent from his pack, which instantly popped open. He had no sooner gotten it over the four of them than the high pitch squealing started as thousands of upset bats flew wildly around the cavern!

Cave In, Cave Out

Bats flew wildly around the tent. "Sorry kids," Tom said. "We won't be able to leave here until the bats calm down."

"How long will that take?" Piper asked.

"Close to thirty minutes," Tom said. "This last year, Mammoth Cave has been experiencing tremors once or twice a month. Usually, it's no problem."

"A tremor causing a cave-in would explain the robber's disappearance," said Peter. "If I've learned anything lately, it's that you have to keep it simple," he continued. "The riddle also says,

'God may giveth but he taketh away.' Maybe they didn't die with the gold. Maybe they were just separated from it and couldn't get back to it. It was taken away from them. Somehow the story of the caves got out even if over the years it became a myth."

"Maybe one of the robbers wrote the riddle," suggested Piper.

Both Peter and Tom looked at Piper in wonder.

"Well," she said. "It's possible, isn't it?"

"Yes it is," Tom said. "And it would explain a lot."

Peter slapped his forehead with the palm of his hand. "It's so obvious," he said.

"What's so obvious?" Tom asked.

"Sanford was the author of the riddle and one of the robbers. He must have known the cave really well. He would have known a good hiding place for the gold," Peter said.

"Where were you guys eight years ago?" Tom asked, smiling.

"I think we were in diapers," Piper said. "So we wouldn't have been much help."

"Do you know if he was missing a friend or family member around that time?" Peter asked.

"Come to think of it," Tom said, "there's a gravesite by the main house that has his cousin's name on it. He died in 1937."

"There you go," Peter said. "He must have been Sanford's accomplice. That fits the part of the riddle that says, 'Look for the treasure where a dead man last sat.' If there was a cave-in it may be impossible to get to the gold."

"You're not giving up, Peter, are you?" Segura asked. "Grandfather would be disappointed in you if you quit so easily."

"Huh!" Piper said. "Peter never gives up! Especially when it comes to pestering me. He's like the Little Engine That Could. Chugga, chugga. Chugga, chugga."

Peter was deep in thought and not listening to his sister.

"Peter!" Piper shouted. "We're talking to you! Earth to Peter, come in."

"Ahh, sorry!" Peter said. "I got lost in thought with something you said, Segura. Remember how your grandfather said he found his way out of the cave after the cave-in that trapped him?"

"Yes," Segura said. "He said he followed Indian symbols our ancestors made."

"That's right," Peter said. "He said they used the symbols to find their way in and out of the caves. They would etch the two symbols into the cave walls just above the floor. A large circle with a line going from the inside to the outside of the circle led the way out."

"So, we already know how to get out," Piper said.

"Yeah," Peter said. "But remember he said he had never seen the other symbol, the one that marked their secret passages that led to other caves they didn't want anyone else to find. The symbol was a large circle surrounding a smaller circle. If I remember right, it meant cave within a cave."

"I've never heard any of this," Tom said. "In all the conversations I've had about the cave with WB, he never told me he was in a cave-in or anything about ancient symbols."

"Can I see the riddle again?" Peter asked. "See the line right here." Peter pointed at the fourth line in the riddle. "'Myth can be fact the Indians do claim, follow their lead for fortune and fame.' See, that fits perfectly. Their lead is the symbol for a cave within a cave."

"But why didn't Sanford use the symbol to find the gold?" Piper asked.

"Good question, Piper," Peter said. "Maybe he was just too overwrought with the guilt of his cousin's death and didn't want anything more to do with the gold."

"So, we have to find the symbol to the undiscovered part of the cave," Tom said.

"Okay," Piper said, fidgeting. "I'm tired of sitting here. I don't hear any more bats. Can we get out?"

"Yes," Tom said, as he turned the tent over to collapse it. "I should take you back to your parents. But you kids have figured out more of the riddle in the last hour than I have in eight years. Did WB say how far into the cave he was before the cave-in happened?"

"He said he had just passed through the second cavern," Segura said. "I have heard the story many times. He said there were two tunnels. He chose the one at the far end of the cavern to go through. It was shortly after that when the cave-in occurred."

The four of them looked at the far end of the cavern. *There was no tunnel!*

A Tunneling We Will Go

"There's got to be a way in there," Piper said, bounding from boulder to boulder in front of where the cave-in had hidden the tunnel.

Tom scratched his head. "Yeah, if we could move a few tons of rocks and boulders!"

"Where's Peter?" Segura asked. "He was here a minute ago."

"He's probably gone and got himself lost," Piper said. "He does that every now and again. I try hard to keep my eye on him, but he usually manages to sneak off and get himself in trouble."

"I'm not in trouble!" Peter shouted. "At least not yet," he added to himself. "I think I've found something."

"Where are you?" Tom asked.

"Behind the large boulder on the left side of the tunnel!" he shouted.

They all ran over to where Peter's voice was coming from. All they could see were his ankles. The rest of him was in a hole not much bigger than he was. Peter backed out of the hole.

"What are you doing?" Tom said. "I'm responsible for your well being, remember. The last thing I need is for you to get hurt."

"I'm okay!" Peter said, smiling.

"Oh, boy!" Piper said. "I know that smile. What did you find?"

"A way to the other tunnel," he said. "The only problem is I'm not sure if it's big enough for Tom to fit through."

"Well, the only way you're going is if I go," Tom said. "So we better see if I can fit." He removed all his gear, including his jacket.

Without his gear, Tom was thinner than he looked.

"How about we go through first, so if you get a little stuck we can wrench you through?" Peter said. "If you can't make it, we'll all come back."

Tom wasn't keen on the idea, but it seemed logical. "Okay, but once you're in the other tunnel don't move more than five feet from the opening."

"Okay, let's do this!" Piper said, but she had a tremor in her voice.

Shake, Rattle, and Roll

Peter crawled slowly through the hole, pushing his backpack in front of him. Before long he was in the other tunnel. He scanned the tunnel. It was larger than the other tunnels. In fact, it was big enough to drive a car through.

"I'm through," he shouted into the hole.

"I'm, I'm almost there!" Piper screamed. There was a little panic in her voice. Peter knew she was afraid of dark, small places. When her hands emerged from the hole, he grabbed them and tugged her the rest of the way.

"Are you okay?" he asked.

"Now I am," she said, clinging to her brother.

Segura was close behind Piper and popped up right after her.

"That was cool!" Segura said.

"Where's Tom?" Peter asked.

"I'm coming!" Tom shouted, as his gear was pushed through the opening.

Just as Tom's arms and head poked through the hole, the ground shook again!

Hang In There!

Peter held onto the girls tightly, as the tunnel floor swayed back and forth. He couldn't tell which one of them was screaming or if it was both. Dust and pebbles fell all around them again. "Close your eyes!" he shouted. But just as he said it, the tremor stopped.

"Are you guys okay?" Peter asked.

Segura and Piper looked at each other as they said in unison, "We're okay."

Peter stared at the hole. His helmet flashlight shined on Tom's unmoving hands. "Tom! Tom! Can you hear me?" Peter shouted.

Tom's little finger moved and then slowly his hands. "Yeah. I hear you. Are you kids okay?"

"We're fine," Peter said. "Can you make it through the hole?"

Without answering, Tom pulled himself forward. His head slowly emerged from the hole and next his shoulders, but then he stopped.

"I'm stuck!" Tom said. "My hips won't go forward anymore. Try jerking me."

Peter took both of Tom's hands in his, and Piper and Segura each grabbed one of his arms. They jerked, they wrenched, they pulled, but Tom didn't move an inch.

"Okay, hold it for a second," Tom said. "The tremor caused the wall inside the hole to move enough where I can't go forward or backward. I need you guys to forget the treasure and find a way out of here to get some help." He paused for a second, catching his breath. "Peter, you're up to bat. Can you do that?"

"Yeah!" Peter said. "We'll find our way out of here. Don't worry."

"Good!" Tom said. "Give your backpack to your sister and you take mine. Just leave me some water and batteries."

Peter did what he was told. "We'll be back as soon as we can. I promise," Peter said.

"I know you will. Now be on your way."

Peter bent down, shook Tom's hand, and nodded. "Hang in there," he said.

The kids held hands, as Peter led them down the big, dark, creepy tunnel.

Cave Within a Cave

Ten minutes later, they emerged into a small cavern less than half the size of the others. No one had said a word.

"I think this might be the cavern your grandfather was in just after the cave-in happened," Peter said. "Spread out and start looking for the symbol."

Peter took the cave wall on the right, close to the tunnel that brought them into the cavern. Piper took the left wall and Segura checked along the front near another large tunnel that led out of the cavern.

"Can't we just go down this tunnel?" Segura said.

"Are there any symbols near it?" Peter asked.

Before Segura could answer, Piper started screaming. Her voice receded into the distance as Peter and Segura ran to where Piper had last been.

"Piper! Piper! Where are you?" Peter shouted, as his light fell on the ancient Indian symbol for a cave within a cave. It was right next to another hole in the wall. This one larger than the one Tom was trapped in.

"I'm okay," Piper yelled. "Come here! You've got to see this!"

Segura went first. The hole was a smooth, wet tube that angled downward for 30 feet shortly after you entered it. Like a water slide, it flattened out at the bottom. Segura screamed all the way down.

Peter tried to walk down it, but his feet slipped, and he slid down the rest of the way. He almost flew right into Piper and Segura, landing on his feet. He couldn't believe his eyes! He was standing on a wide ledge, 10 feet above a fast-moving underground river.

"Isn't that cool?" Piper said.

"Yeah," Segura said. "This cave is amazing!"

Peter looked around. There was no way off the ledge! There was no path! No connecting tunnel! No ledge to walk along! Nothing! The only choice of exit was a slick tube or a ride down the river.

"Piper," Peter said. "Why did you want us to come down here?"

"Duh?" Piper said. "Just look at how cool this is."

"Did you think about looking around for a way out before calling us down here?" Peter said.

Piper looked around her. "Uh, oh!" she said.

Peter felt it before the girls did. He grabbed them, pulling them close to him.

"What's..." Piper started to say when she suddenly felt the tremor, too.

CCRRRAACCCKKK!

Peter looked down and saw a crack forming along the ledge where it met the wall. "HANG ON!" he shouted, as the ledge broke free.

Surf's Up

The girls didn't have time to scream before they plunged into the cool water. They all resurfaced at the same time, as the rushing current kept the ledge from pulling them under. After their initial shock, the ride downstream was like a lazy river ride at a water park.

Peter was having trouble staying afloat because of the weight of Tom's pack. He unstrapped it and let it go, then turned around to face the girls. "We have to find our way out of here before the water gets colder. Keep your eyes open for anything we can grab."

Just as he said that, Piper pointed behind him. "Like that?"

Peter turned to see an old rope strung across the river. "Grab for it!" he shouted, as he reached out of the water. His hand snagged the rope. Segura and Piper reached for it, but Piper's reach wasn't long enough. Peter reached out with his other hand and snagged the strap of his backpack that Piper was wearing. He yanked her back with all his strength. This time she managed to reach up and grab the rope.

"Follow me," Segura shouted, as she moved along the rope hand over hand toward a wide ledge that ran along the right-hand river wall. After climbing onto it, she helped Piper and then Peter.

They laid there, exhausted.

Shhh! Listen!

"I guess all those gym classes came in handy," Segura said.

"So who was it that always gets us in trouble?" Peter asked Piper.

"Okay, one time it's me," she said. "But all the other times it was you."

"You know," Segura said. "I haven't had this much fun with any of the other kids that have stayed at the campground. You guys have kept me from having a boring summer."

"Glad we could be of assistance," Peter said. I wonder what the Indians hid over there, he thought. Hmm! That's a mystery for another day.

"So," Piper said. "What do we do now?"

"We keep moving," Peter said. "It will help dry us out and keep warm."

The ledge disappeared into another tunnel and then it opened up into a gigantic cavern. The river, although not as wide at this point, ran down the middle of it.

"Great!" Piper said. "Another cavern. Too bad the bats in here can't lead us out."

Peter stared at his sister.

"What?" Piper said. "What did I say now?"

"Piper, what you said was brilliant!" Peter gently removed the wet postcard from his pocket. "There were three sections of the riddle that stumped me, but I think I know what they mean." He looked at the riddle. "'The river winds through this cavern of shame.'" We're in the cavern of shame right now," Peter said, pointing at the river.

"Does that mean we're close to the treasure?" Segura asked.

"Possibly," Peter said. He continued to read. "'Look for the treasure where a dead man last sat, find him hidden with the eyes of a bat.'"

Piper scanned the cavern. "Ahh! Silly rabbit, I don't see a dead man lying about, and how are we going to find the treasure with the eyes of a bat, anyway?"

"I think the question should be, 'What are the eyes of a bat?'" Peter said.

Segura suddenly started jumping up and down, raising her hand. "I know, I know!" she all but screamed. "They're his ears!"

"Correct," Peter said.

"Okay," Piper said. "That still doesn't help us, Peter. I know your ears are a little on the pointy side, but they're a little small. Where are we going to get bat ears and how are we going to see with them? We don't have echolocation."

"No we don't," Peter said. "Plus, our ears aren't as sensitive as a bat's." Peter went behind Piper and opened his backpack. He pulled out his "Listening Post" and removed it from the large zipper bag he had put it in.

"What's that?" Segura asked.

"It's a parabolic microphone," Peter said. "It can pick up sounds from a distance or enhance sounds close by."

Peter put in the ear buds and pushed the power switch. He pointed it back at the tunnel they had come through. He heard a soft swooshing sound, like wind. As he moved it along the cave's perimeter, he noticed another tunnel he hadn't seen before. It had the same swooshing sound. The tunnel looked like it headed back in the direction they had come. "Peter," he heard softly.

"What?" he asked, looking at the girls.

"What, what?" Piper said.

"Why did you...?" Peter heard the voice again. "Piper, can you guys hear me?"

The Eyes of a Bat

The voice was getting louder. "It's Tom, I hear him calling our names in that tunnel over there!" Piper squealed.

They all ran to the tunnel, shouting. Suddenly, Tom limped through the tunnel entrance into the cavern. The girls ran to him and hugged him. Peter shook his hand. "How did you get free?" he asked.

"That last tremor loosened the rock around me and I was able to pull myself the rest of the way out of the hole. However, I twisted my ankle in the process," Tom said. "I was worried it might have hurt you guys. Why are you guys wet?" he asked.

"Piper took us in a different direction to get here," Peter said, pointing at the river.

Tom limped his way toward the river. "Oh man! This is incredible; it's part of the riddle. We must be close to the treasure. But we can't risk it anymore, we have got to get out of here before there's another tremor."

Peter explained to Tom what they were trying to do.

"Okay!" Tom said. "But you've only got ten minutes. Then, gold or no gold, we're out of here. I don't want you guys in any more danger."

Peter was again moving the microphone along the cave walls. He completed one full turn. Other than the two tunnels and the river, there were no other sounds. Nothing! Then suddenly he got an idea.

"Clap!" Peter said.

"What?" Piper asked.

"Clap slowly and together," Peter said. "I want to see if I can pick up an echo like the eyes of a bat."

The girls and Tom began clapping methodically, while Peter slowly spun around in the cavern. He picked up the echo on the walls but not when he aimed at the tunnels. As he moved around, there was a slight ripple in the echo. He moved the microphone back, and there it was again.

"Keep clapping but follow me," Peter said, strolling toward the portion of the cave where the sound had changed. They got five feet away from the wall and he still didn't see anything.

Four feet.

Three feet.

And there it was!

Gold Rush

"It's an optical illusion," Tom said. "From a distance it looks like one wall. But when you're right on top of it, you see there are two different walls. It's like the front black curtain on a stage blending into the back black curtain on the wall a short distance behind it."

"Yeah!" Peter said. "I'm sure the fact that they're only a foot apart helps them to blend even better."

Piper squeezed through the opening.

"YIIIIII!"

Peter and the others rushed through the opening and rounded a short bend. Lying on the ground before them was a skeleton. A large bag of gold coins sat where the man's lap once was.

"I can't believe it!" Tom said with a gasp. "After all these years of searching! Bats is going to be so surprised." His eyes scanned the area around the skeleton. There were five more bags of gold coins. He picked up a coin and looked closely at it. It was a 1933 double eagle, one of the rarest gold coins in the world.

"You did it, Tom!" Peter said. "You discovered a treasure, that according to the government, never existed."

"No!" Tom said. "You guys did it. Without you..."

"We all did it together," Piper interrupted. "Teamwork, like Mom's always saying. No man is an island unto himself."

Segura brought them all back to reality. "This is great, guys, but we're still trapped. How are we going to find our way out of here?"

"Not a problem," Peter said, smiling.

The Great Escape

Peter strolled up the tunnel Tom had come through, moving his microphone from side to side, while he scanned the floor for WB's ancient exit symbol. Tom, Piper, and Segura were just a few steps behind him.

"WB never mentioned an underground river," Peter said. "Which means he never got this far. So the hole he escaped through has to be in this tunnel between here and the small cavern where we took our detour down the lazy river."

"You'll have to tell me about that one after we get out," Tom said.

"Knox-Knox," Piper said.

"Not again," Peter said. "You've got to learn to pace yourself, like only one KnoCK-KnoCK joke per vacation. Besides, can't you see I'm trying to concentrate?"

"I always pace myself. I don't tell more than I think you can bear," Piper said. "Knox-Knox."

"I'll do it!" Segura said. "Who's there?"

"Wooden."

"Wooden who?" Segura asked.

"Wooden you like to know where the exit is," Piper said.

Peter suddenly heard the swooshing sound of wind and stopped. He looked at the wall and there, near the floor, was the exit symbol. Tree roots hung down the wall like vines on a castle wall.

"I think this is it," Peter said, rushing to the wall and pulling the roots aside. There, in front of him, was a hole big enough for each of them to climb through.

"Knox-Knox," Peter said.

"Who's there?" Segura asked, before Piper could.

"Ben," Peter said.

"Ben who?" Segura asked.

"Ben looking for it and here it is. Tada!" Peter said, holding the roots aside so they could all see the hole. "Who said you can't mix ancient Indian symbols with modern electronics?"

Peter looked at his sister. "Let's go home," he said.

"Yeah," Piper said. "I wonder what Mom's making for dinner. I'm so hungry I could even eat—bat poop!"

The others laughed. Just then a small spec of white guano fell on Piper's forehead. She reached up and swiped and stared at the white smear.

"EEEEWWWW!" she said.

Her brother laughed. "The expression on your face, Piper, is pure gold!"

THE END

Postlogue

A bright full moon lit up the night sky over Breadloaf. The campsite was already cleared and everything was packed away. Breadloaf was hooked up to the SUV, ready to head for home. Mom wanted to drive at night to avoid the daytime traffic.

It was time for them to go, and Mom, Dad, Tom, Segura and Piper stood near the SUV saying their goodbyes. Peter crawled around the SUV, lurking sinisterly, never tiring of playing vampire ...

About the Author

Carole Marsh is an author and publisher who has written many works of fiction and non-fiction for young readers. She travels throughout the United States and around the world to research her books. In 1979, Carole Marsh was named Communicator of the Year for her corporate communications work with major national and international corporations.

Marsh is the founder and CEO of Gallopade International, established in 1979. Today, Gallopade International is widely recognized as a leading source of educational materials for every state and many countries. Marsh and Gallopade were recipients of the 2004 Teachers' Choice Award. Marsh has written more than 50 Carole Marsh Mysteries™. In 2007, she was named Georgia Author of the Year. Years ago, her children, Michele and Michael, were the original characters in her mystery books. Today, they continue the Carole Marsh Books tradition by working at Gallopade. By adding grandchildren Grant and Christina as new mystery characters, she has continued the tradition for a third generation.

Ms. Marsh welcomes correspondence from her readers. You can e-mail her at fanclub@gallopade.com, visit the carolemarshmysteries.com website, or write to her in care of Gallopade International, P.O. Box 2779, Peachtree City, Georgia, 30269 USA.

Built-In Book Club

Talk About It!

1. Who was your favorite character? Why?

2. What was the scariest part of the book? Why?

3. Would you like to go spelunking? Why or why not?

4. Why do you think Peter thought the gold at Fort Knox should be stored in a bank instead of a secret vault? Discuss some reasons for saving money.

5. Piper knew that Segura was an American Indian because of her unusual name and pigtails. What is the difference between respecting other cultures and judging someone by their appearance?

6. If you found a treasure, how would you use it?

7. Peter said that vampire bats do not normally bite humans. Does this change your mind about bats being scary? Why or why not?

8. What was the funniest part of the book?

Built-In Book Club

Bring it to Life!

1. Let's go on a treasure hunt! Ask each book club member to hide a secret surprise somewhere. Then have each member draw a map to their surprise using the ancient Indian symbols from the book. Don't forget to tell them how to get back to their starting place! Good luck treasure hunting!

2. Get Batty! Have each member of the book club research a different type of bat and present what they learned to the rest of the group. Then, discuss some reasons why most people are afraid of bats.

3. Are you ready to go spelunking? Have each member of the book club create their own spelunking kit with a bottle of water, a helmet, a

flashlight, and some extra batteries. When each member has their kit assembled, use your flashlights to find some treasure!

4. Create your own parabolic listening device! You will need a clean, empty vegetable can and some long pieces of thin rope (long enough to stretch across a room). Ask a parent to drill a small hole into the bottom of the cans. Then, tie two cans to each other with one long piece of rope. Pick a partner and stand at opposite sides of the room. You'll be able to hear your partner talk like he or she is right next to you!

Write six pen pal postcards. Write three to a bat...and then answer them!

Bat Trivia

1. Bats have a thumb and four fingers just like people!

2. Bats will only bite someone out of self defense.

3. A single brown bat can catch more than 1,000 mosquitoes in an hour!

4. Some bat mothers have been known to adopt orphan bats.

5. Bats are the only mammal that can fly!

6. The bumblebee bat is the world's smallest bat and weighs less than a penny!

7. The brown bat can live more than 32 years!

8. Bats are nocturnal. They sleep during the day and eat at night.

9. Bats hang upside down when they sleep!

10. There are nearly 1,000 types of bats all over the world!

Mammoth Cave Trivia

1. Mammoth Cave is the longest cave in the world! The temperature stays at 54 degrees all year.

2. The Kentucky cave shrimp in Mammoth Cave don't have any eyes!

3. There are 350 miles of passageways and five levels in Mammoth Cave!

4. There are about 130 different types of tiny species living in Mammoth Cave.

5. When you visit Mammoth Cave, you'll probably see more crickets than bats!

6. The Green River has five types of fish that are not found anywhere else in the world!

7. You can go spelunking at Mammoth Cave! There are cave tours just for kids like you.

Fort Knox Trivia

1. Fort Knox is home to the U.S. Army Armor Branch Headquarters and the U.S. Bullion Depository, or the "Gold Vault."

2. More than $6 billion worth of gold is stored in the Fort Knox Depository!

3. Fort Knox is so big that it is considered a certified city in Kentucky!

4. After WWI, the U.S. Army used Fort Knox to train soldiers how to drive tanks!

5. Visitors at the Fort Knox Depository can stand outside the gate and take pictures, but they are never allowed inside.

6. A single gold bar stored in Fort Knox weighs about 27.5 pounds!

7. Parts of the James Bond movie "Goldfinger" were filmed at Fort Knox.

8. Important documents like the Declaration of Independence and the U.S. Constitution were stored at Fort Knox until 1944.

9. The vault door that leads to the gold at Fort Knox weighs more than 20 tons!

10. Fort Knox was named after Henry T. Knox, a general in the Revolutionary War.

Glossary

bequeath: to give, hand down, or leave in a will

bullion: a bar of gold or silver

depository: a place that holds money that has been deposited by others

elude: to escape or avoid something

embellish: to decorate or add details to something

guano: bat droppings

harrowing: terrifying or extremely painful

negligent: to be careless or irresponsible

oblivious: when someone is not aware of the things around them

spelunking: the exploration and study of caves

Pen Pal Fun

Do you have a pen pal? It can be a lot of fun, and you can learn a lot, too!

Why you might like to be a pen pal:

1. Make a new friend. You might even be friends for life!

2. Improve your writing and reading skills.

3. Learn how people live in another town, state, or country.

4. Share thoughts and ideas with someone your own age.

5. Look forward to getting the mail every day—there might be something for you!